W9-AXM-285

FRANKLIN PARK PUBLIC LIBRARY
FRANKLIN PARK, ILL.

Dairy Farm Doozie

Written by Barbara Buzaldua
Illustrated by Sue DiCicco

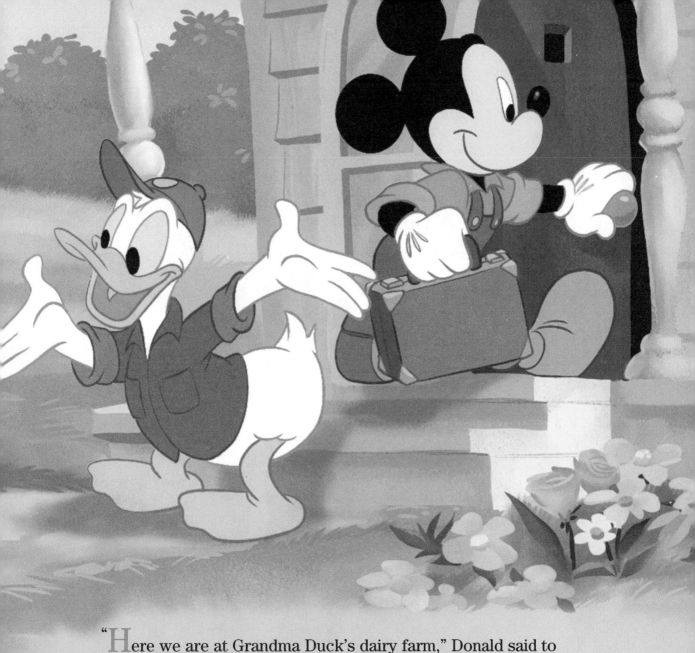

"Here we are at Grandma Duck's dairy farm," Donald said to his nephews Huey, Dewey, and Louie one summer morning. Mickey was with them, too. They had all promised to take care of Grandma's cows while she was on vacation.

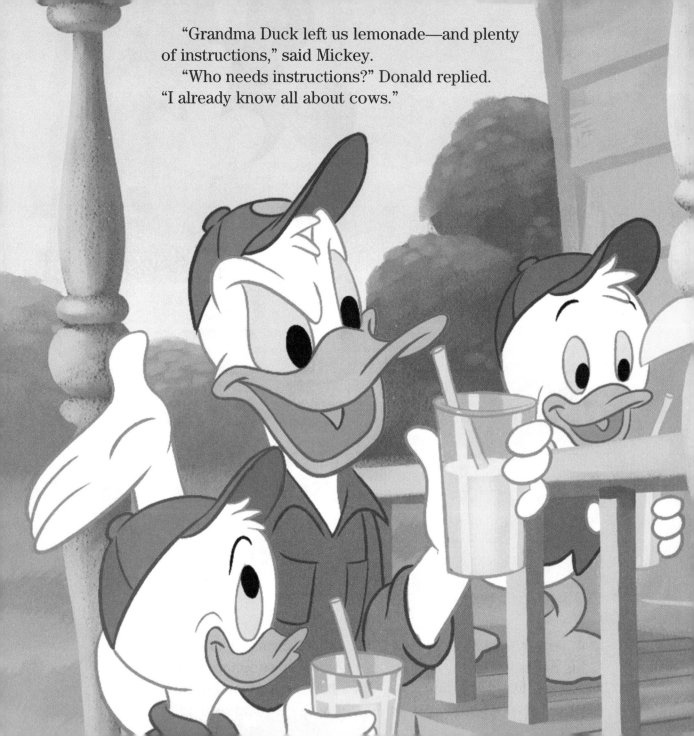

"Grandma Duck left us lemonade—and plenty of instructions," said Mickey.

"Who needs instructions?" Donald replied. "I already know all about cows."

Mickey read Grandma's list. "It says here to milk the cows in the morning, put them out to pasture to eat grass, and then take them to the barn for their evening milking."

"I knew that," Donald said. Whistling a cheerful tune, he headed for the pasture. Mickey followed with Huey, Dewey, and Louie.

Mickey and the boys found the cows drinking from the farm
pond. Mickey gave the largest one a gentle pat to get her started
toward the barn. The other cows followed.

Donald saw one last cow standing behind a big, round bale of
hay. "Here, cow, here, cow!" he called. But the cow wouldn't come.

"I said, 'Here, cow!'" Donald yelled, stomping toward the big animal.
Mickey, Huey, Dewey, and Louie hurried over to see what was
happening. There, next to the big cow, stood a little calf.
"Why, this must be Rosie and her new calf!" Mickey exclaimed.
"Grandma mentioned them specially in her instructions."

"Grandma says to take Rosie's calf to the barn and help it drink from a bottle," Mickey said.

Donald tried to lead the calf in the direction of the barn. But Rosie blocked his way.

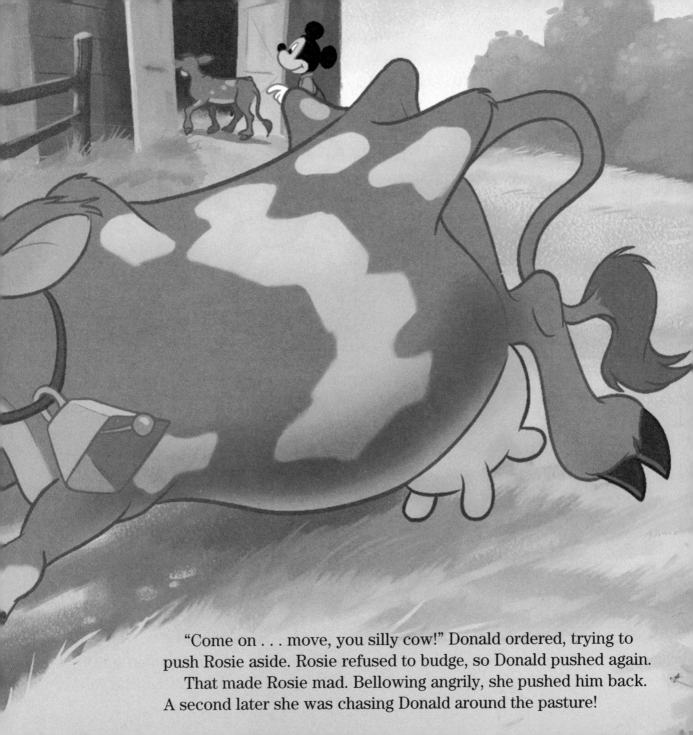

"Come on . . . move, you silly cow!" Donald ordered, trying to push Rosie aside. Rosie refused to budge, so Donald pushed again. That made Rosie mad. Bellowing angrily, she pushed him back. A second later she was chasing Donald around the pasture!

Meanwhile, Mickey and the nephews had led the little calf to the barn and fed it from the bottle. Then they put the calf in a straw-filled stall.

"When Donald gets Rosie into the barn, we'll milk her. Then she can snuggle with her calf," Mickey told the boys.

Just then, Donald dashed into the barn with Rosie close behind him.
He raced into a milking stall with Rosie right on his heels. Donald slipped
away from the big cow, slammed the stall door shut, and leaned against it.
"Guess I showed *her* who's boss!" he said, wiping his forehead.

"You sure did!" Mickey agreed. He handed Donald a bucket of soapy water. "Now you can wash her before she's milked."

"Aw, phooey! Who ever heard of washing a cow?" Donald muttered. But he lugged the bucket into Rosie's stall.

Donald set the bucket down right behind Rosie.
Swish, swish! went Rosie's tail as she flicked it back and forth.
Plop! went the tail as she dipped it into the soapy water.
And *whap!* went the tail as Rosie smacked suds right in Donald's face!

Sputtering and muttering, Donald finally managed to get Rosie washed. He watched Mickey and the boys hook the other cows up to the milking machines.

"Now, *that* looks easy," he said. But when he tried it with
Rosie, she pushed him over and started to run.
"Whoa!" Donald shouted, grabbing her by the tail.

"Watch out, Unca Donald!" Huey shouted as Rosie dragged Donald through the barn. Donald's feet got tangled in the hoses that carried the milk to the storage tank.

Snap! One of the hoses came loose. Milk sprayed everywhere, soaking Donald from head to toe and splashing in his eyes.

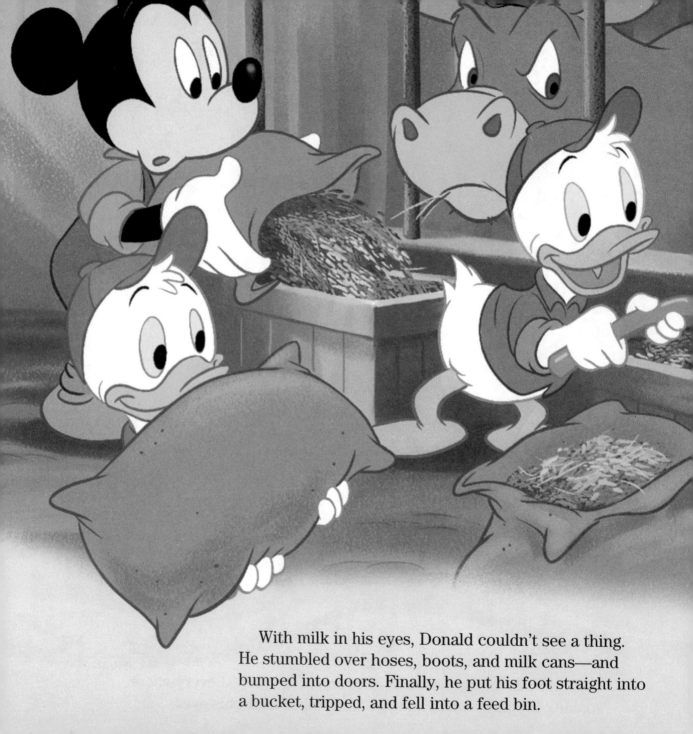

With milk in his eyes, Donald couldn't see a thing.
He stumbled over hoses, boots, and milk cans—and
bumped into doors. Finally, he put his foot straight into
a bucket, tripped, and fell into a feed bin.

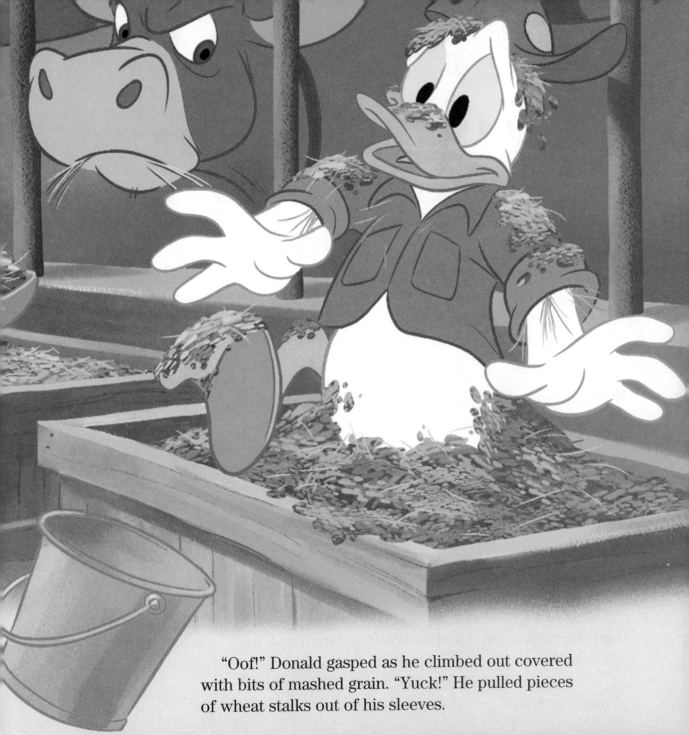

"Oof!" Donald gasped as he climbed out covered with bits of mashed grain. "Yuck!" He pulled pieces of wheat stalks out of his sleeves.

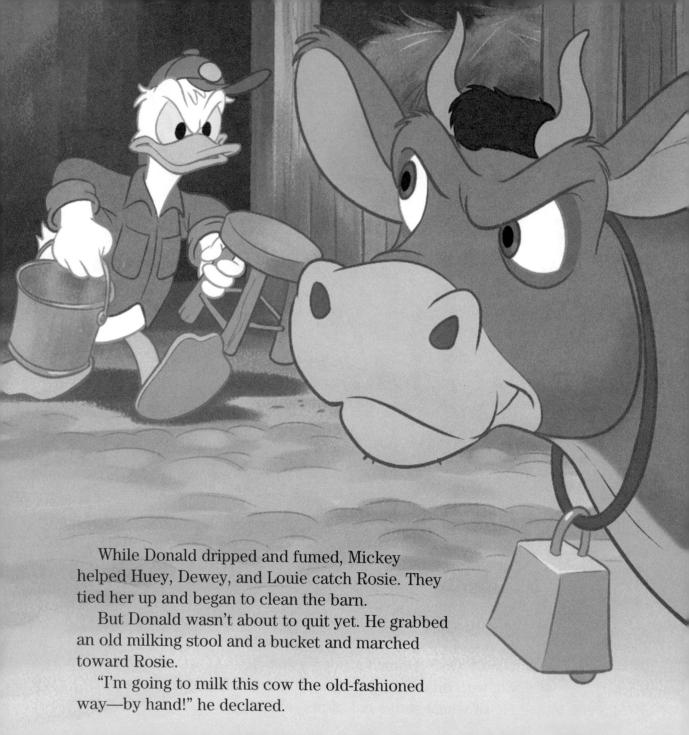

While Donald dripped and fumed, Mickey
helped Huey, Dewey, and Louie catch Rosie. They
tied her up and began to clean the barn.

But Donald wasn't about to quit yet. He grabbed
an old milking stool and a bucket and marched
toward Rosie.

"I'm going to milk this cow the old-fashioned
way—by hand!" he declared.

When Rosie saw Donald approaching, a sly glint came into her big brown eyes. As soon as he got close enough, she gave a powerful kick—*thunk!*—and sent him flying through the air. Donald landed—*splash!*—headfirst in a full milk can!

Mickey pulled Donald out of the can. "You've helped enough for today," he said, trying not to smile. "We'll finish milking Rosie."

Rosie stood contentedly while Mickey milked her, and then Huey, Dewey, and Louie easily led her to the box stall with her calf.

After their chores were finished, the gang trooped back to
the house and sat down for a rest on the front porch.

Just then, Grandma Duck drove up. "I missed my cows too
much to stay on vacation," she explained.

"Hmph! I hope I never see another cow again as long as I live!"
Donald said grumpily.

"That's too bad," Grandma said. "Look what I brought you."

She handed each one a box. When they saw what was inside,
everyone began to laugh—even Donald. For in each box was a
huge piece of milk chocolate, shaped just like a cow!